Richard Carpenter's

ROBIN OF SHERWOOD

THE BARON'S DAUGHTER

I0618598

Richard Carpenter's
Robin of Sherwood
The Baron's Daughter
By Jennifer Ash
Published in 2025 by
Chinbeard Books

in association with
Oak Tree Books
oaktreebooks.uk

Editor: Barnaby Eaton-Jones
Sub Editor: Harriet Whitehouse

Cover shows Peter Hutchinson as Alan a Dale and
Stephanie Tague as Lady Mildred de Bracy, with
Clive Mantle as Little John, Claire Toeman
as Meg, and (obscured) Michael Praed as
Robin Hood and Judi Trott as Marion.

Richard Carpenter's

ROBIN OF SHERWOOD

THE BARON'S DAUGHTER

by

Jennifer Ash

A Chinbeard Books / Oak Tree Books Original

This story is set some time after *The Enchantment* from Series 2 of *Robin of Sherwood*.

PROLOGUE

The blazing warmth of the great hall's fire should have been welcome after three days in a cold damp cell, but Alan a Dale was too frightened to appreciate its enticing glow of orange heat.

Dragged by the shoulders, his legs limp as his boots scuffed a pattern in the dusty floor, the minstrel had been deposited at the feet of Baron William de Bracy by two heavy-handed guards. Waiting anxiously for whatever fate was about to befall him, Alan's gaze darted around the dimly lit hall in an attempt to look anywhere other than at the anger-puffed face of his father-in-law.

The Baron, however, had other ideas.

Reaching down to his prisoner, the nobleman's mailed fist shot forward and tightened around Alan's throat. 'I trust a stay in my dungeon has given you time to think through your situation.'

Spluttering against the pressure of the older man's grip as he was hauled upwards, Alan could do no more than miserably stare into the cold black eyes of one of the most powerful men in England. A second later, he was thrown back to the floor.

The minstrel, once the Baron's household entertainer, massaged his throat as he thought of Mildred, his wife of just six months (who also happened to be Baron de Bracy's daughter). The last time he'd seen her, in the Scottish manor house where they'd found work as a pair of balladeers, Mildred's face had been alight with happiness. But now… Alan closed his eyes against the visions of terror that confronted his imagination every time he considered what his wife might be going through.

He didn't even know where she was.

After the planned marriage of his daughter, Mildred, to the Sheriff of Nottingham had been thwarted by the notorious outlaw Robin Hood, so that she could marry a mere minstrel instead, de Bracy was further enraged by Hood feeding the peasants of Sherwood on the proceeds of Mildred's dowry. He had employed mercenaries to track the young couple down. It had taken six months, but the Flemish cutthroats had eventually proved their worth in gold. Literally.

Satisfied that Mildred was in safe-keeping, miles from where her pathetic excuse for a husband now stood riddled with fear, the Baron poured himself a goblet full of wine. He sipped it slowly, savouring the sight of his terrified son-in-law as much as his drink's silky-smooth texture.

As de Bracy refilled his goblet, his temper got the better of him once again and he slammed the vessel against the table, making Alan yelp with nervous anticipation as the blood-red contents slopped everywhere.

Growling with barely suppressed menace, the Baron spat, 'I *repeat*; have you considered your position?'

Shuffling his feet, his eyes downcast, Alan mumbled, 'I— I have, my Lord.'

'My daughter would be less than flattered to hear you sounding so unsure when her life hangs in the balance.'

'Her… *life*… my Lord?'

Relishing the startled expression on Alan's face, de Bracy's palm slapped the table next to him. 'Yes, her life! What do you think that's worth to me now she has disgraced the name of de Bracy by marrying a peasant? *Well?*'

Raising his hands beseechingly, Alan pleaded, 'My lord, we were happy together and—'

Frustrated by the boy's blind naivety, the Baron interrupted. 'Happiness means *nothing*. You were always a pitiful minstrel, now I discover you're a foolish dolt as well.'

Struggling not to let his whole body shake, Alan meekly enquired, 'Where *is* Mildred, my Lord?'

Still suffering from a hunting injury he'd received just before his daughter's aborted marriage which had damaged his leg so much he now had a permanent limp, de Bracy failed to conceal a wince as he got to his feet. Furious and unblinking, he shoved his face as close to Alan's as possible and peered blankly into the minstrel's worried eyes. 'My daughter is under lock and key at Welbeck Abbey, far away from her unholy union with you.'

Recoiling from the stench of the Baron's sharp breath, Alan half expected the man to yank a dagger from his belt and dive it straight into his heart, as he stuttered, 'Our marriage was far from unholy. Friar

Tuck himself conducted the ceremony. A respected cleric!'

The laugh that shot from the Baron's lips was entirely devoid of humour. '*Respected cleric?* The fact that this union was blessed by an outlaw—who has, in all likelihood, been excommunicated—is *nothing* to be proud of. It probably means you are not actually married at all and have been living with my daughter in a state against the teachings of the church!'

'*No*, my Lord! I can assure you, Friar Tuck was…'

'BE QUIET!'

Baron de Bracy sat back heavily against his chair, making the old wooden seat creak beneath his weight. Watching as Mildred's father stretched out his damaged leg, Alan fidgeted, his growing state of nervous tension making him unable to stay still.

After what felt like a lifetime, de Bracy gripped his chair's arms and, leaning forward, spoke with a crisp, calculated anger. 'If you ever want to see Mildred again, then you will do what I say.'

'Yes, my Lord.'

'You will travel into Sherwood, find Robin Hood and lure him to Welbeck Abbey. Tell him you need help to rescue Mildred from her cell there. I hear he's always ready to help people—although I can't think why.'

Horrified at the notion of betraying the very man who'd helped him rescue Mildred from a loveless union with the Sheriff of Nottingham, Alan trembled as he asked, 'Why, my Lord?'

'So my men can do what Robert de Rainault has repeatedly failed to do: capture the outlaw who helped my daughter escape a marriage I worked so very hard to secure.'

Alan was wondering how he'd even begin to find the Robin Hood in the vast range of Sherwood Forest all on his own, not to mention get to an abbey he'd never been to before, when the Baron bellowed across the hall so hard that the candles on the table before him guttered.

'I *will* get revenge on this hero to the poor who humiliated me, stopped my daughter's wedding and stole her dowry!'

Seizing the chance to make the Baron less angry with both him and the outlaws, Alan spoke fast, hoping his courage wouldn't fail him. 'B— but, my Lord, Robin Hood did *not* steal the dowry. I swear it! The Sheriff tricked everyone and kept the ten thousand marks for himself. He had no love for Mildred or marriage. He wanted to wed lands and riches, not *her*.'

In the sudden hush that followed, all that could

be heard was the crackle of the low fire in the grate and the movement of a few servants on the other side of the hall.

The Baron's bearded face creased into deep thought. 'Why should I believe you?'

'Because I speak the truth, my Lord!' Alan held his breath, his heart hammering in time to the footfall of a guard crossing the hall behind him, as he waited for the Baron to respond.

Abruptly, with a measure of control that was in complete contrast to the roar Alan had been expecting, de Bracy clambered up from his chair to his feet and clapped his hands together twice. Two men-at-arms immediately ran to his side.

'Guards! Undo this man's shackles and find him a mule.'

Then, twisting on the spot, the Baron levelled his eyes on his son-in-law. 'You *will* lure Robin Hood to Welbeck Abbey, minstrel, or you will watch Mildred die. Now get out of here!'

Alan's teeth chattered, part from fear of the man before him, and part from a new sense of helplessness. 'Die… but… but how will I..? My Lord, I…'

The minstrel's words faded to nothing as the two guards slipped their arms under his, and towed him bodily from the hall.

As soon as Alan a Dale had been unceremoniously dismissed, the Baron sank lower into his seat and muttered into his replenished cup of wine. 'Robert de Rainault, you promised me you would marry my daughter, and that is precisely what you are going to do. After all, soon she will be in want of a new husband, and I would hate Mildred to be a widow for very long.'

CHAPTER ONE

Despite being comfortably entrenched in a deep mattress of straw, Friar Tuck couldn't sleep. Rolling his bulky frame onto his back, he stared up at the barn roof. He could just see the early morning sunset creeping its way through a few cracks in the wood.

Tuck knew he should be feeling content. Invited by the townsfolk of Worksop to help rid them of an over-ambitious tax gatherer, the outlaws had been successful in teaching the money-grabbing leech a long overdue lesson on the dangers of intimidation. They had sent him on his way with his money bags empty, a bruised ego, and the forthcoming nightmare of having to tell the Sheriff of Nottingham he'd lost the King's money. But, nonetheless, Tuck was troubled.

With a creak of straw and rafters, he moved onto his side. Nasir and Marion slept soundly in the straw next to him, the snuffling and occasional snore coming from them demonstrating that they were enjoying the luxury of having a roof over their heads.

Tuck turned to Much who, unlike their companions, was sat up, his eyes trained on the doorway below. 'How can they sleep so soundly?'

'They're tired, Tuck. So am I…' Much yawned, as if to prove the point, '…but I want to see when Robin gets back.'

'Don't worry; he'll be back as soon as Herne has spoken to him.'

Much didn't turn his head away from his vigil. 'I wish John and Will were here.'

The friar gave a heavy sigh. 'So do I, Much, but ever since Gisburne spotted John coming out of Meg of Wickham's hut, he's been watching the village like a hawk. John's afraid to leave the place unguarded.'

'Why didn't Will come, then? He'd have been handy when we were teaching that tax gatherer a lesson.'

Suddenly exasperated as well as tired, Tuck found himself explaining the situation to his young friend for what felt like the tenth time. 'Because Robin didn't want to leave John protecting Wickham alone. Now, try to get some sleep. I promise to wake you when Robin gets back.'

As Much did as he was told, snuggling back into the hollow he'd made in the straw, Tuck mumbled under his breath, 'Whatever you are asking of your son, Herne, I do wish you'd ask him a little quicker.'

Tuck turned over again, levelling his eyes upon the rickety ladder which led to the barn below. He tried to relax, but months of living in the forest had sharpened his senses… and right now every single one of them told the cleric that something was wrong.

Uttering up a silent prayer, Tuck whispered into the night, 'Where *are* you, Robin?'

The birdsong which had accompanied Robin of Loxley as he'd stood in the clearing with Herne died away as the Lord of the Trees passed him a small cup and bid his son to drink its contents.

Obeying at once, Robin grimaced at the sickly sweet yet gritty taste. As if from nowhere, it seemed,

Herne then produced a large shallow bowl. Holding it out before him, he beckoned his son to come closer.

'*What do you see?*'

Robin's head spun. He sank into a dream-like state and images began to form as he stared into the depths of the bowl.

Once the strange purple mist that had shrouded the bowl cleared, Robin muttered quietly, narrating the changing scenes that appeared before him.

'A pale female hand rests flat against a smooth stone wall… A fallen shield of blue and yellow with a plain betrothal ring bouncing off it, as if thrown in anger rather than dropped…' He licked his lips as the pictures changed fast, too fast for him to take in every detail. 'A flash of a white robe… and…' He closed his eyes as he heard a voice coming from the depths of the vision and realised it had been there from the very start. It was the sound of singing. Robin reopened his eyes, but the pictures had gone; all that was left was the song. 'It's a woman's voice, sorrowful and alone.'

As the tune faded, the purple mist thickened, regathering across the bowl's surface, making Robin blink. Only once the bowl was nothing more than a workaday vessel again did Herne speak.

'*Prevent a wrong you have already righted.*'

Robin stared straight into shrewd eyes that were almost hidden beneath the antlered headdress the forest spirit wore.

'"*A wrong we've already righted*"? What does that even mean?'

But the Hooded Man's question went unanswered, for Herne the Hunter had already gone, fading into the forest as if he'd never been there.

Sitting on a fallen tree trunk, Robin massaged his forehead. The drink Herne had given him to stimulate his vision made his temples thud. Closing his eyes against the burgeoning morning light, he considered what he'd seen.

I swear I've seen that shield before... but where..? and that voice... do I know it?

Robin sighed. He wanted to get back to the heart of Sherwood. Although he was still cross with Little John for disobeying him and continuing to visit Meg of Wickham at nighttime, Robin was also worried about his friend.

Now that Gisburne had, personally, seen John leaving the village under the cover of darkness, there was no way he'd rest until he'd either caught John or made the village pay for harbouring one of Robin's men. Although they could have done with both Little John and Will Scarlet's help to teach the local tax gatherer a lesson, he didn't begrudge Wickham having their protection for a few days.

I hope you two can manage, as it doesn't look like we'll be straying far from this part of the forest yet. Whatever Herne was trying to tell me, I'm sure this is where we'll find out.

Hauling himself to his feet, Robin hooked his bow over his shoulder and, checking around him to make sure the path was clear, he broke into a run, heading back towards the barn.

CHAPTER TWO

The Abbot of Welbeck was a troubled man. Already out of favour with the Crown for sharing the abbey's money with the poor—rather than handing it over to help pay for the French wars—he hadn't dare refuse when one of King John's most influential nobles had asked a favour of him.

No. That wasn't true.

The Baron de Bracy had *demanded* a favour of him, threatening his future existence—and that of his abbey—should he not do what he'd been told.

'Dear Lord, forgive me. I feel I've failed in my role as abbot… but I didn't know what else to do.'

Giving an involuntary shudder, the Abbot rushed along the corridor, the sound of his sandalled feet hitting the stone floor echoing with each step.

He made his way to a locked stone room, weighing a key in the palm of his hand.

Even before he had reached the heavy wooden door that temporarily barred the occupant from the world, he could hear her. The sound of her singing leaked through the walls of the cell.

'Her father has seen her locked away, yet still she sings. My one comfort is that the girl seems content. It's as if she's waiting for someone.' He swallowed, lifting his eyes as if to address Heaven whilst he hovered outside the cell. 'Give me the strength to help her as best I can Lord, Amen.'

The Abbot paused to listen as his captive's voice rang out anew, each word clear and true. This was a melody he hadn't heard before. The girl sang neither of saints nor kings as one might expect from a young woman of breeding, but of felons and mischief. She sang balladeers' tunes.

> *Once I met an outlaw brave,*
> *a man all garbed in green.*
> *His life he cares not about,*
> *he fights the sheriff, mean…*

The Abbot clutched at the wall to steady himself, his countenance pale. 'Dear God in heaven. The Baron was right, she *has* met Robin Hood!'

Tired and weary, Alan a Dale trudged through Sherwood. At first, he'd felt full of hope—turning his mission to save his love into a story he could eventually sing as he rode. But as each hour passed, and the early morning turned the corner that heralded the coming of noon, the charm of the birdsong and the rustle of the leaves had begun to wane.

He was becoming desperate, and the mule he'd been given to ride upon had long since given up being co-operative.

'Come on, you stupid mule! You're supposed to carry *me* into Sherwood. So far I've dragged you nearly all the way myself!'

Trying to ignore the voice at the back of his head that told him he'd been going around in circles, the minstrel became increasingly tense. With every tiny movement he flinched, his ears alert for danger, his songs—for once—stilled on his tongue. Suddenly, he stumbled to a halt. 'What's that? Oh, a bird! Where *are* you, Robin?'

Moving on again, concentrating on the time

when he'd be reunited with Mildred, Alan heaved on the mule's lead, pulling it forward again until a crunch of leaves told him that this time, his imagination wasn't playing tricks on him—there really was someone nearby.

'Who's that? Oh… thank goodness…' Alan relaxed as he realised he'd heard a villager heading home… and not just to any home. To the place he'd been aiming for.

'Look, you feeble steed, we've arrived! That's Wickham over there, so Robin Hood can't be far away.'

Alan's heart lifted. He wasn't worried about leading the outlaws into trouble with the Baron; he'd convinced himself Robin's men were of stout enough heart to overcome any evil that lay before them. He smiled as he began working on a ballad that would sum up their next adventure.

'It will be an epic of daring and close calls with danger, before—heroically—the fair damsel will be saved from the clutches of a mailed fist, and… *Ahhh!*'

Alan ducked down behind the mule as two figures appeared from between the tress, frightening the life out of him. His expression of terror, however, quickly turned to joy as he found himself face-to-face with a couple of the very people he'd been looking for.

'Little John! Will Scarlet!'

'Alan? What the devil are you doing here?' John asked in surprise.

'I've made it. Saints be praised!'

'What? *All* of them?' Will Scarlet's eyes narrowed as he stared to either side, making sure the minstrel was alone.

'I've travelled so far to find you,' Alan beamed. 'It's like a song! The hero starts full of hope, then there is despair… but then, no! He succeeds in his quest, and—'

Fearing that their companion might burst into song, John hurriedly said, 'Come on, Alan. Let's have a warm by the fire.'

'What do you mean they're in Worksop?' exclaimed a shocked Alan.

What do you think we mean?' muttered Will Scarlet, 'They're. In. Worksop,' he added pointedly, already fed up again with Alan, who'd he'd barely tolerated the first time around.

'I must get Robin's help, or the Baron will kill Mildred!' Alan stared at the two outlaws from across the fire, his eyes filling with tears of frustration. He couldn't believe his bad luck.

'Aye, we understand. We really do. But—' started Little John, before being interrupted by the no-nonsense Scarlet at his side.

'It's only a two-hour ride north,' he stated, and then glared at Alan's mule, rubbing the bite he'd received from the animal when he'd tried to lead it to a tree and tie it up, 'Or perhaps four on that stubborn beast.'

Rather than jumping into action and setting off on a new journey, Alan buried his head in his hands instead. He wailed in despair, which initially gave Little John and Will Scarlet a bit of a start, then made Scarlet whisper under his breath to John, 'He sobs like he sings. Terribly.'

The minstrel didn't hear him as he cried out a reason again for needing Robin's help, 'But Mildred is in terrible danger!'

Will Scarlet took his eyes off the offensive mule and the offending minstrel and fixed them on the forest road ahead, ever on the alert for Gisburne's men—especially with the loudness of Alan's woe punctuating the normally quiet Sherwood air. His reply to Alan's utterance was textbook Will Scarlet, who had little time for self-pity and even less time for the simpering Alan. 'Well… Alan,' he said, 'You'd better get a move on, then!'

Little John, always the eventual peacemaker when it came to his impatient friend, unhooked the reins of a horse that they'd recently acquired from an unwitting and unfortunate soldier who had bumped into the two outlaws earlier, offering them to the minstrel.

'Take this horse, lad. It'll be faster than that feeble beast. And, no, I'm not talking about you, Will.'

'Eh?'

'Follow the road to Worksop,' continued Little John, 'and you may well meet Robin on his way back. I'm sorry we can't go with you.'

'Yeah, we got Sherwood folk to look out for,' Scarlet added.

Getting to his feet, Alan pushed his shoulders back in an act of what he felt was courage, wiped his eyes with his sleeve, and instantly became full of a new determination to find his wife. 'Thank you, Little John. I shall include your kindness in my next song.'

'I can hardly wait,' grimaced Little John, in what he hoped was an encouraging smile and not a rictus grin.

With Little John's apology for not accompanying him—and Will's unsympathetic murmurings of having their own people to look after—ringing in his ears, Alan rode his newly-gifted horse northwards towards Worksop.

Keeping to the right road as Little John had suggested, Alan hadn't got very far before he heard the pounding of horses' hooves, ridden at speed. He decided to swerve his own mount deep under the cover of the trees and off the road, as he didn't know who was approaching, though it sounded like a speedy bunch.

Alan drew in a sharp breath as the heavily armed soldiers galloped past him. This was somewhat due to the pace at which they were riding, but more so because he recognised the men's livery—and he was glad he had stayed out of sight.

They were from de Bracy.

And they were galloping towards Nottingham.

CHAPTER THREE

Robert de Rainault, Sheriff of Nottingham, groaned as he opened his eyes to find himself confronted by the gloating face of Sir Guy of Gisburne.

'Hell's teeth, Gisburne, can't a man have a hangover in peace?'

'I'm sorry, my lord.'

'I do not appreciate being shaken awake before noon, you know that!'

Rolling over and pulling his bed covers with him, the Sheriff's attempt to fall back into a semi-comfortable slumber was immediately thwarted by the urgent pleading of Gisburne.

'You have visitors, my Lord. They are… insistent.'

'Are they now?' sighed the Sheriff as he sat up and passed an unsteady hand over his forehead, letting out a sharp wince. 'Well, let them wait awhile. Pass me my robes!'

With an attempted smile, Sir Guy passed the Sheriff his clothes and waited.

'And, for God's sake, stop standing there, Gisburne. Your mere presence is making my headache worse. Go and breathe somewhere else. Or, better still, stop breathing!'

As his deputy gave a low bow, his now-amused grin still firmly in place, Robert de Rainault yanked his tunic over his head before swinging his legs out of bed and tugging on the rest of his garments. 'I suppose we'd better get this over with.'

As he tiptoed through the castle, every step increasing the thump in his head ten-fold, the Sheriff found himself constantly having to dodge his many servants as they dashed around, completing their duties as quietly as they could.

By the time he had reached the Great Hall, Gisburne at his heel, de Rainault was in an even more foul mood—a rising temper made more terrible by the sight of the four heavily-armed men awaiting him by the fire. Worse still, one of them was sprawled nonchalantly in his chair—his *favourite* chair.

He sped up, his anger at the impertinence of this newcomer outweighing the pain of his claret-caused hangover.

'What is the meaning of this invasion?' De Rainault began, but his words faltered, and his manner took on a miraculous transformation from anger to acceptance. He'd noticed the rampant boar insignia that adorned his visitor's cloaks. 'Ahh, you've come from the Baron de Bracy?'

'Indeed we have, my lord.' The Baron's Captain of the Guard tapped an authoritative hand on the arm of the Sheriff's chair as he sat straighter, appearing every inch a man who knows he has the upper hand. 'His Lordship has recently discovered that Robin Hood did *not* steal his daughter's dowry, after all.'

The Sheriff's lips were already dry, but they somehow now felt drier.

'He believes,' continued the Captain, 'that you kept it for yourself.'

Ignoring the tiny sniggering snort that escaped from Gisburne, the Sheriff snarled back, 'How dare you!'

Unmoved by the display of petulance before him, the Captain slowly rose from the chair. 'This is a matter that the Baron de Bracy wants sorting out. You are to come with us at once.'

With a gleeful look on his face that he didn't bother to disguise, Gisburne made a play at reassuring his master. 'I think you'd better go with them, my Lord. Don't worry, I'll look after Nottingham.'

Wincing as his stomach lurched, reminding him how much wine he'd drank the night before— and how little food he'd consumed to help soak it up—the Sheriff gave a muted growl, 'You could at least try to hide your delight at this preposterous situation, Gisburne!'

'Come, Sheriff! It does not pay to keep my master waiting.' De Bracy's captain adjusted his cloak, making sure the rampant board emblem was clear for all to see. 'Men, I think the Lord High Sheriff of Nottingham may need our help.'

If Gisburne had made another snide remark, the Sheriff didn't hear it, for suddenly he was engulfed by the visiting guards, all of whom had clearly been chosen for this task by virtue of their size and strength. As a variety of mailed fists grabbed him, Robert De Rainault found himself tripping over his own feet, and his head rhythmically pounding as he was ushered from his great hall at a most efficient speed.

'Hey! Take your hands off me, you oaf!' He struggled as his slight frame was sped towards the castle gates, shouting as he went. 'I can walk on my own, you know... Ouch! Do something, Gisburne...'

'There's only one sensible way to deal with this, John,' Will Scarlet kept his voice down as—from the safety of the trees—he watched the villagers of Wickham go about their business.

'And what way would that be, lad?'

'Hard, fast and final... then we can get after Robin, because I don't trust that tax gatherer one bit.'

John felt a rush of guilt. If Gisburne hadn't spotted him coming out of Meg's hut, they would be with the others anyway, helping teach one of the Sheriff's hired lackeys a lesson.

'They'll be on their way back now. Five of them will easily have dealt with him—*and* returned the money to the people.' Lying on his stomach, his head in his hands as he watched Edward of Wickham talk to his wife on the other side of the village, John added, 'Although, I did think they'd be back by now.'

'Exactly—they should be, and they ain't.'

'If anything's happened to them because—'

Will shook his head. 'No good thinking like that, John. You know you ain't supposed to stay with Meg, but you did. End of story; lesson learnt. If something's 'appened, you'll have to live with it.'

'Yeah, I know.' John scrubbed a hand through his thicket of unruly hair, his gaze never leaving the village, as Will Scarlet went on.

'There's been no sign of Gisburne *or* that smarmy Captain of the Guard, so I say we give it until nightfall tomorrow—then, if he don't show, he's not going to. Yes?'

'Right.' John swallowed back an image of what Gisburne might do to Meg if he and his men arrived after their backs were turned, but he knew he couldn't stand on guard here forever, not when so many other people needed their help. 'So—if they do come—then how would your "hard, fast and final" idea work? There's only two of us.'

'I know that!' Will's frustration at the situation ignited his short temper. 'But better just the two of us than the villagers getting involved and Gisburne having another stick to beat them with.'

'Aye, alright!' John grumbled. 'I don't need to be made to feel any worse than I do!'

As the reduced band of outlaws walked through the northern reaches of Sherwood, Marion slipped a hand into her husband's palm. 'Where are we going, Robin?'

'I don't know. All I know for sure is that we can't go back to the camp yet. Not until we've put right the wrong Herne showed me.'

Not sure why Robin was so convinced that the prophecy he'd seen meant they had to stay near Worksop, Much's innocent expression was etched with concern. 'But what about John and Will, Robin? They're at home on their own.'

'I know, Much, but Herne said…' He tailed off, as he could see how tired and confused Much was. 'Look, let's rest here a while and I'll try to explain.'

Coming to a halt beneath a clump of trees, Robin took the water pouch from his belt and sat between the tree roots. As Marion, Tuck and

Much joined their leader on the forest floor, Nasir positioned himself in a low branch of the nearest tree, automatically acting as lookout while Robin fully relayed the message from Herne.

As soon as Robin had finished, Tuck asked, 'The white robes you mentioned seeing, was there anything distinctive about them?'

'I only saw a flash of them. It was more an impression of someone wearing them. And all the time there was the faint sound of singing… a woman, I think.'

Shuffling his bulk in an attempt to get more comfortable, Tuck took a draught of water. 'We aren't far from Welbeck Abbey you know; an hour's walk, maybe. It is home to a group of Premonstratensian canons.'

Much coughed as he tried to get his tongue around the word, 'Premonstra— what?'

Tuck laughed kindly, 'They're a religious order dedicated to St James the Great, Much. They wear white robes.'

'Like monks?'

'Yes Much, just like monks.'

Patting Tuck heartily on the back, Robin leapt to his feet. 'That has to be it! Let's go to Welbeck.'

Rather than jumping up to join him, Marion

stayed where she was. 'And if it isn't the abbey that Herne meant us to go to?'

'Then we keep walking until we discover where he *did* mean us to go. Which way is the abbey, Tuck?'

Shrouded on one side by the forest of Sherwood—and open to the countryside on the others—the high stone walls of the Abbey of Welbeck glinted in the midday sunshine. The bell to noon prayers sounded as the outlaws caught their first glimpse of the impressive building.

Hiding themselves amongst the trees opposite the gatehouse, Robin pointed to a coat of arms placed high above the wide gatehouse door. 'This *is* the right place. Look. It's divided into two halves. That's the shield Herne showed me.'

Relieved they were in the right place, Marion asked, 'What do we do now?'

'We can watch the gatehouse from here.' With a rising feeling that time wasn't on their side, Robin turned to Nasir. 'Will you take a look around, Nasir? I want to know if anyone else has been here recently.'

'I will check.'

As the Saracen slipped between the trees, Robin took a moment to think. 'The only reason Herne would have led us here is to help someone. We have to get inside the abbey. If it's the girl that I heard singing who needs us, she'll be in there.'

'We can't just walk into an abbey though, Robin.' Much gnawed on his bottom lip as he stared at the imposing stone structure.

Nobody needed to say how foolish—not to mention dangerous—it would be for Robin Hood to walk into an abbey. Even though they'd never had dealings with the place before, they all knew how far word of their exploits in Sherwood had spread.

'I could go.' Tuck patted at his tonsure.

Marion peered out across the open grass that separated them and the gatehouse. 'If they have a girl in there, they are more likely to let me near her than Tuck. We should both go.'

'Thank you, Little Flower. That does seem a sensible course of action.'

Robin wasn't so sure, 'They may well know who you both are.'

Friar Tuck shrugged through his smile, 'Maybe, but perhaps they won't. Either way, we have to try; otherwise, why would Herne have sent us here?'

'You're right. Thanks, Tuck.' Robin hugged Marion to his chest. 'If you can hear any singing, then head towards it.'

Marion laughed, 'It's an abbey, Robin, there's *always* singing.'

'But this will be a single female voice. It should stand out amongst a house of canons easily enough.' He looked towards Tuck, 'What will you tell the abbot?'

The cleric gave a mischievous grin, 'I have an idea about that, but Marion might not like it.'

'Why won't I like it?'

'Come on,' Tuck winked playfully as he left the safety of the trees, ready to set off across the clearing towards the abbey, 'you'll see.'

As their friends moved away, Much called softly after them, 'Be careful.'

CHAPTER FOUR

Although the Baron de Bracy had told the abbot to expect a visit from Robin Hood, it was still a surprise to see two of the outlaw's followers talking to the abbey's porter.

Taking a deep breath, hoping the warmth of his greeting appeared genuine, the Abbot opened his arms wide in welcome as he hastened across the chilly stone floor.

'No need to trouble me with fake introductions; I know who you are. Friar Tuck, Lady Marion—I am honoured to make your acquaintance.'

A surprised Marion glanced at Tuck. 'You are, my Lord Abbot?'

Privately wondering how long he could keep up his fake demeanour, the Abbot led them to his study. 'Why would I not welcome those who strive to do good in the world? Let's take some refreshment whilst you tell me how I may help you.'

Pouring wine for his guests, the Abbot gestured for them to take a seat.

Positioning his corpulent frame onto a hard wooden settle, Friar Tuck readied himself to make his request—pointedly avoiding Marion's gaze as he spoke, for fear that the lie he was about to utter would earn him a sharp poke in the ribs.

'Father, I have come to ask for a room for the Lady Marion. Robin is soon to face a most villainous enemy. Quite understandably, he fears for his wife's safety, and I have been charged with her care. If you, my Lord Abbot, would be kind enough to provide overnight accommodation for her, we would be most grateful.'

'Gladly. If only every request was so easy to grant.' The Abbot clapped his hands. 'Finish your drink and I'll show you to a guest room. You are welcome for as long as necessary, my Lady.'

'Thank you, my Lord Abbot,' Marion spoke demurely, before swiftly drinking her wine and rising to her feet.

A few minutes later, the pair were being led through Welbeck's many corridors towards a chamber which, the Abbot explained again, Marion was welcome to use for as long as she needed.

'Let's see if I can find the right key.' Producing a bunch of keys from his belt, the Abbot searched through them as they walked. 'Yes, here we are.'

Coming to a halt, he slipped the chosen key into the lock and swung open the door to the guest room, just as the sound of a woman singing in the next room reached their ears.

> *'His truth was pure,*
> *the fighter of those who'd*
> *trap a flower beneath a glove*
> *and kill a season in the bud…'*

Soft and true, the verses filled the room, bewitching them all, making them stand still so that they could listen.

Seeing Tuck's troubled expression, Marion turned to the Abbot. 'What a beautiful voice. You have another guest?'

The Abbot gave a sorrowful nod. 'Enchanting, isn't it? Sad, though. The room contains a young novice waiting to go to our sister priory in Lincolnshire. Her abbess has requested a period of total solitude for her, before she takes her final vows.'

A trickle of anticipation ran down Marion's

spine. Keeping her tone calm, she mused, 'Perhaps she is in two minds about her future.'

The Abbot of Welbeck stared at the locked door. 'Perhaps…'

As the afternoon waned, a breeze ran through Sherwood, carrying with it the sound of a horse plodding between the trees; it was accompanied by an off-key song, its mournful delivery doing nothing to improve the melody.

> *'My heart is heavy as a stone,*
> *My tears they fall like rain,*
> *For she who is my own true love,*
> *I'll never see again…'*

Alan a Dale had given up trying to be quiet as he rode through Sherwood. He was too sick of heart to care who heard him now. Robin and his men were nowhere to be found, and Mildred was lost to him. All he could do was throw himself at the mercy of the Abbot of Welbeck. Adrift in misery as he approached the abbey, Alan abandoned his love song and started singing a tale he'd written for Mildred.

> *'I go in search of Robin Hood,*
> *a man so wise and brave,*
> *to save a dove of white skin pure,*
> *from the life of a slave…'*

The minstrel's song soon collapsed into a pitiful sigh, 'Oh, fair steed, I have failed to find Robin and failed to save my beloved wife.'

Hidden between the trees, Nasir felt the approach of a horse and rider before he'd truly heard them.

'Someone approaches.' His eyebrows rose, as a badly sung ballad reached his ears. However unexpected the lyrics of the song were, he knew well the lips that delivered the ill-keyed music.

'There is only one person who could kill a tune so easily.'

Nasir was tempted to let the minstrel blunder on by unheeded, but then remembered Herne's message about the outlaws righting a wrong that they'd righted before. *We've helped this minstrel before. Could we be meant to help him again?*

Emerging from the shadows, Nasir appeared

before the startled minstrel and bowed low. 'Alan a Dale. You were looking for us, perhaps?'

Having taken his leave of Marion and the Abbot, Tuck hurried back to the edge of Sherwood. His face glowed red with effort as he puffed his way across the open area of grass that fronted the abbey and ducked beneath the welcome shelter of the trees.

Robin lowered himself from an ancient oak tree, while Much emerged from between a nearby set of closely-placed ash trunks.

'What happened, Tuck? Is Marion safe?'

Not waiting to catch his breath, Tuck glanced back the way he'd come as he replied to Much's urgent enquiry. 'The Abbot was welcoming. He knew who we were. I asked him to let Marion have a room while we dealt with a dangerous situation. Thankfully, he didn't ask what that situation was.'

Robin couldn't help but laugh as he imagined his wife's reaction to the implication that she couldn't have coped with any of the dangerous situations they often found themselves in.

'And Marion didn't punch you? I myself haven't

recovered from being hit by that branch when I suggested she shouldn't fight with the rest of us.'

Shaking his head, Tuck chuckled as he recalled the time in the village of Elsdon—not long after he'd had the pleasure of joining his friends in wedlock—when Marion had been less than pleased to be told she couldn't fight alongside the men because she was a girl. 'Nothing's forgotten!'

Much shifted anxiously from one foot to the other as he asked, 'Did you find the singing girl, Tuck?'

'That I did, Much; that I did. She's in the room next to the one the Abbot gave Marion. He said she was a novice considering her place in the world before taking her final vows.'

Robin held Tuck's gaze. 'But *you* don't think that was true, do you?'

'Judging by the words the lass sang, I'd say if she is a novice, then she'll be leaving Holy life before taking the wimple.'

Unease prickled at Robin's palms. 'You said the Abbot was friendly.'

'I know what you're thinking. Too friendly, perhaps? I'm not sure.' Tuck took a water pouch from the small stash of supplies they had with them, and drew a healthy glug.

Remembering the swish of white robes in his vision, Robin said, 'It seems too much of a coincidence that he took Marion to the room right next to the person we're looking for.'

'It could have been the only room available. How are men of the church supposed to react when a known female outlaw arrives on their doorstep seeking refuge?'

Much peered anxiously at the abbey gatehouse. 'Are we going to have to rescue Marion as well as the girl now, Robin?'

The friar patted him on the shoulder. 'Don't worry, Much. Marion hasn't been locked in.'

Robin's lips curved upwards. 'Tuck, are you suggesting that the Abbot placed Marion in that room so that she could help the girl escape.'

'It crossed my mind.'

Suddenly the image of a ring being thrown against a shield ricocheted through Robin's mind, and his smile dissolved. Herne's vision had warned him that it wasn't going to be that easy. 'Then we have to assume Marion will try and free the girl.'

Much was puzzled. 'But she might not want to come with us, if she wants to be a nun?'

'Bless you,' Tuck ruffled Much's hair, 'but I don't think she's *really* a novice.'

'But, you said the Abbot said—'

Much's words died on his lips as a crunch of leaves and the sound of a single horse being ridden through the trees behind them made them freeze.

'Shh! someone's coming.'

As Robin reached for Albion, a familiar face appeared. 'Nasir! It's not like you to make a noise…' His words faded as he saw that the Saracen was not alone. He was leading a horse by the bridle upon which sat a man the outlaws hadn't seen for almost six months.

'Alan! What are you doing here?'

Even as he asked the question Robin knew the answer. Herne's words resounded through his mind. *The right they'd already wronged…* 'Mildred's locked in the abbey, isn't she?'

Alan opened his mouth in surprise. His delight at having been found by Nasir, morphed into awe. 'Yes, yes she is. How did you know?'

'Never mind that now,' Robin urged, 'how did this happen? You and Mildred were on the way to Scotland when we last saw you.'

Alan's face lost its colour as he told them how the Baron de Bracy had hired Flemish mercenaries to track him and Mildred down. Not deterred by the Scottish border, the mercenaries had located the manor where the two had found work as balladeers. As he spoke, Alan lapsed into his storyteller style, making Robin wonder how much the tale had been embroidered for extra impact since the events described had happened, though he soon realised that the embroidery was so embedded that only the most delicate fingers could have managed it.

'One night, they broke into the manor—there were at least twenty of them, all tall and broad with evil in their sunken eyes, screaming mine and Mildred's name—and they seized us with such fiery rage that I feared our hair would be set alight and our skin melted away. Mildred was lifted over the shoulder of the biggest mercenary and taken off in a waiting carriage, all the while her tiny fists pounding on this brute's back.

'I did try to stop it happening, but I was beaten about the head with what felt like an anvil, thrown into chains that weighed heavier on me than the sins of Hell itself, and bundled unceremoniously into a nearby wagon like a sack of grain. I passed out after that, not waking until I found myself in the dankest of dungeons—so wet and dark, that you would think it had been dug far underground, and that a special long ladder would have been commissioned to be able to descend into it.

'After what seemed like weeks—though perhaps could have been mere hours—without my basic needs of food, water and the tender touch of my Mildred, I was hauled up out of the dungeon and dragged like a dead animal to the castle's hall. There I found myself face-to-face with Mildred's father, the Baron de Bracy. He spat venom at me, stabbing cruel words into my heart like the pointiest of pointy daggers. My ears buzzed, stinging with pain as each new attack flew around my head like a swarm of vitriol. He declared our marriage nothing more than fakery, because it was conducted by an outlaw who had been disowned by Church and King.'

The minstrel took a deep breath and sighed. Robin wasn't sure whether they all should give him a round of applause, but he looked so miserable that Robin feared he would either cry or burst into song, if they did. Neither prospect appealed. 'How did you know Mildred was here?' he asked, instead.

Nasir, who'd been listening with increasing disbelief at the elongated story, broke his usual silence to add, 'And how did you get out of de Bracy's castle?'

Flushing pink, Alan blustered, 'Baron de Bracy. Oh, that evil baron. He forced me to tell him *everything*, and now he is angry—filled with a temper that overflows like a waterfall—with the Sheriff of Nottingham as well.'

Much's eyes widened, 'He's angry with the Sheriff? Why?'

Alan nodded miserably, 'The Baron wants his dowry back.'

'I bet he does!' Robin snorted, 'But that doesn't explain how you escaped, Alan, or how you knew that Mildred was in Welbeck Abbey?'

'I was in the hall of the castle, pleading with the Baron to spare Mildred's life. That was when I told him about the Sheriff having the dowry. That evil fiend had convinced the Baron that *you* had stolen it, Robin.'

Friar Tuck tutted, 'How convenient,' he said, as he struggled to listen to Alan's continuing tale of woe.

'The Baron flew into the wildest of rages. He shouted about Mildred being here—at Welbeck Abbey—and under lock and key, so I slipped quietly away while he was threatening to get revenge on the Sheriff. I was more stealth-like than a fox, quieter than an owl swooping for its prey, as delicate as—'

Robin interrupted, before Alan could compare himself to another animal, 'You knew you had to get to me for help, is that right?'

Alan nodded.

'But why?'

'You have no fear,' Alan explained.

Robin was speechless for a moment, before asking, 'How can you possibly believe I fear nothing?'

'You have proven it many times!' Caught up in the drama of his explanation, Alan pleaded, 'You *have* to help me save Mildred. I cannot be the hero of this story, for I am not brave like you. I need to be her Prince, and you her winged steed. You told me, Robin, that life wasn't a love song. But it *is*, don't you see?'

Robin looked at Tuck in despair as he tried to explain. 'Alan, we do what we believe to be *right*. It doesn't mean we aren't afraid, and it doesn't mean we always *get* it right either. We have lost people along the way. Lost friends. It is hardly a love song.'

'But...'

Before Alan could press his point, Nasir interrupted with a paucity of words that Alan could only dream about. 'Evening falls soon. We must go inside.'

Switching his gaze back to the sky above the gatehouse, Robin knew Nasir was right as he pondered the situation. 'You are right, Nasir, but... if the Abbot isn't all he seems, entering the abbey could be dangerous as well as disrespectful. We should give Marion time to get the girl out.'

With a barely perceptible dip of agreement, Nasir murmured, 'But not *too* much time.'

As Robin and Nasir silently watched the abbey, Much sat down on the grass, and beckoned the minstrel to join him, 'How did you find us, Alan?'

'I went to Wickham. Will Scarlet and Little John told me you were near Worksop. I was heading that way when I happened upon Nasir. Or he happened upon me.'

The friar smiled, 'Our friends are well?'

'Hearty and kind, Brother Tuck. They lent me this horse and—' Alan abruptly stopped talking; his gaze now firmly fixed on the abbey. 'Listen…'

On the edge of the light wind, faint but audible, they could hear a perfectly pitched voice singing.

Alan jumped to his feet.

'Mildred! It has to be her. It just must be…'

CHAPTER FIVE

Marion sat on the side of the compact bed. The small but comfortable room reminded her of the chamber she'd been given in Nottingham castle during the tedious years she'd spent as Abbot Hugo's ward, before Robin had taken her to live with him in Sherwood. 'Although,' she conceded to herself, 'this place is much more peaceful.'

She began to pace as she heard a gentle song seep through the walls.

'There must be some way of taking the girl out unnoticed. If I wait until the canons are at prayer then…' Suddenly, she stopped moving. 'I *know* that song!'

Marion moved closer to the connecting wall, holding her ear to the stone.

> *'My heart is heavy as a stone,*
> *my tears they fall like rain,*
> *for he who is my own true love,*
> *I'll never see again, again…*
> *I'll never see again…'*

'Alan a Dale sang that song! This girl must be Mildred!'

Returning to sit on the edge of the bed, Marion pictured the young couple she and her fellow outlaws had helped escape from a cruel father and—potentially—crueller husband.

As the volume of the ballad became louder, she settled herself down to wait.

At last, after what seemed like an eternity, the prayer-call to Vespers rang out and Marion opened her unlocked door. Peering left and right, she could see no one. *The monks must all be at prayer.*

Creeping forward to the neighbouring cell, Marion tried the handle of Mildred's door.

'It's locked. Of course it is. It couldn't be easy, could it? Now what?'

Peering around her, making sure there was still no one in sight, Marion risked a hushed shout, her face planted against the door. 'Mildred! Can you hear me?'

Before she had the chance to listen for an answer, hurried footsteps approached Marion from behind, making her heart lurch as she spun around.

Bracing herself to throw a punch, Marion's arm was halfway back before she realised it was the Abbot, and she hastily lowered her fist.

'May I help? The door is so thick, she'll never hear you.'

Marion didn't hide her surprise. 'Abbot! You made me jump.'

'Forgive me, but I assumed you had come to get the girl out. Here, let me help.'

'You were expecting us?'

The Abbot slid a key into the lock, his hands trembling. 'I've been hoping someone would come for her. But... er... if anyone asks, I will tell them I was overcome by outlaws.'

'Thank you, my Lord Abbot. You are a good man.'

Passing Marion the key so he could say it had been stolen from him, the Abbot explained the strain on his conscience since Mildred's father had ordered the imprisonment of his youngest child at Welbeck, before hurrying away. 'Good luck, Lady Marion. I must join my brothers at prayer.'

Mildred was huddled on the bed, her arms wrapped protectively around her knees. She blinked when she saw the door open—and again as she recognised the woman who poked her head around the door. 'Marion! Is that really you?'

'It is.'

'Has Alan sent you?'

'Come on, Mildred. Hold my hand, we must move quickly… and *very* quietly.' With a reassuring smile, Marion picked up the girl's travelling cloak and threw it at her. 'Hurry, we don't have much time.'

Wishing their booted feet didn't sound so loud against the stone floor, Marion kept alert as they moved cautiously towards the gatehouse. Hoping she'd been leading them in the right direction, Marion experienced a surge of relief when she recognised the entrance hall through which she and Tuck had been guided earlier. But, just as they turned towards the gatehouse, they found the Abbot waiting for them. His face was a picture of misery. A soldier held his arms fast behind his back.

'I'm so sorry Lady Marion, Lady Mildred… I had no choice; the Baron said…'

As Marion saw who stood beside the Abbot, she moved in front of Mildred. She kept a gentle but firm hold of the shaking girl's arm.

'I think they can see the situation for themselves, Abbot.'

Mildred gaped in horror. 'Father! What are you doing here?'

De Bracy completely ignored his daughter as his men surrounded the women. Giving a derisive grunt, he slowly reached up and picked a bright yellow and blue shield from the wall, before throwing it to the ground.

'You show your colours with pride, Abbot, but they are worthless.'

As the metal shield continued to rock against the stone floor, the Baron grumbled to himself, 'When will I learn how foolish it is to trust a man of God?'

Abruptly, lunging forward, de Bracy grabbed his daughter's right hand, and stabbed a finger at the wedding band she wore. 'Take that pathetic ring from your finger.'

Tilting her chin upwards, Mildred whispered, 'I will not.'

'If you don't, then I will see it chopped off— finger and all. It is about time you wore a more fitting ring on that hand, daughter.'

Knowing her father was not one for idle threats—and that he was quite capable of removing her finger himself there and then, in any way he chose—Mildred yanked her hand away from his, and removed the ring herself.

'Here! Take it. You can't take away what it means though, Father.'

'Look at it,' de Bracy scoffed, 'Cheap and nasty, just like the man who gave it to you. It's fit for nothing but the dung heap.'

Before Mildred had the chance to stop him, her father threw Alan's betrothal ring with force against the shield.

'No! Don't throw it away. I want—'

'What you *want* is of no concern to me.' De Bracy spun around, fixing his black eyes on Marion of Sherwood. 'Now, you—outlaw wife. Where is

Robin Hood? Don't waste your breath by pretending you came here alone.'

'He awaits me in the trees beyond the abbey.'

'Alone?'

'Alone.'

Suddenly shuffling forwards from the shadows into which he'd hastily shrunk, the Abbot of Welbeck's voice shook as he said, 'Please, my Lord, Hood is there, but he is not alone. He has a friar with him.'

Marion gasped in horror at the betrayal, as the Abbot—shaking from head to foot—continued, his expression hot with shame. 'It would be foolish to lie to him now, my Lady. The consequences could be… terrible.'

'Where the hell have you been!?' Will Scarlet hissed, as Little John returned.

'The camp! You know that.'

Will tutted loudly. 'I thought you'd gone via London! You've been ages.'

John dropped the long coil of thin rope onto the ground before them. 'Well, next time, *you* can go. That's heavier than it looks.'

'What? Too heavy for the Giant of Sherwood?' Will winked as John sank to the ground and picked up a flask of ale.

'Any sign of Gisburne?'

'Nothing.'

'Maybe he won't come. You know what a short attention span he has.'

'Maybe he will, maybe he won't—but I want to be ready, just in case.' Scarlet peered up at the sky. 'If he *is* coming, I reckon it'll be before he prepares to stick his snout into his evening meal.'

John began to stretch out the weighty rope that he'd lugged across Sherwood. 'Do you think Alan reached the others?'

'If he didn't get lost,' Will sighed. 'I dunno— but I've got a really bad feeling about all this. I just can't stop thinking that they're walking blindly into something more dangerous than a greedy tax man, now that the minstrel has turned up again.'

Turning back to look at Wickham as its people stirred, ready to face the long day ahead, Little John agreed. 'We'll stick to the plan—if Gisburne hasn't arrived by this evening, we'll head to Worksop.'

CHAPTER SIX

The outlaws waited restlessly on the edge of the forest. Time had dragged since Friar Tuck had returned without Marion, and Alan's erratic behaviour was not helping. One minute, the minstrel would be loudly confident that Robin, Nasir, Much and Tuck were capable of helping him overcome any obstacle to get Mildred back. The next, he'd need an almost gushing landslide of reassurance that his wife would be alright. He was up and down more often than the notes in the songs he sang, and not in a pleasant way.

As the breeze through the trees dipped in temperature, Robin—tired of inaction—had outlined a plan he'd put together.

'It's agreed, then. If there's no word from Marion

by the last toll of the bell that ends Vespers, then we will enter the abbey.'

They were still impatiently waiting for Marion and Mildred's appearance when the abbey's bell did finally begin to sound. Silently, Robin nodded to his companions. Picking up their swords, they were about to leave the safety of the shadows when Nasir held up a hand and they all stopped moving.

'Too late. Look!'

A scuffle from the gatehouse—the first rumblings of which Nasir had heard—grew louder and caught their attention. The door was thrown open with speed, and several men-at-arms piled forward, their swords drawn.

Tuck wiped a hand over his troubled face. 'Where did those soldiers come from? I saw none inside.'

Robin gripped Albion, his trusty blade, a little tighter. 'Shame,' he sighed, 'the Abbot was obviously hiding something, after all. His true colours, for a start.'

Nasir had shimmied up the nearest tree to get a better view. 'Eight men,' he declared.

'And Marion?'

Nasir paused briefly before replying. 'At the back, Robin. One guard grips her.'

Alan a Dale thrust his hands to his hips as he glared across the clearing. Robin had a horrible feeling he was about to make a stirring speech about how they could save the day, but then, suddenly, the balladeer's hands fell to his sides. An expression of despondency crossed his face as two people emerged from the centre of the gathering. Two people he immediately recognised: one he loathed, one he loved.

'The Baron!' he exclaimed, 'Oh no, he has Mildred! I must get to her, and—'

Leaping to the ground, Nasir grabbed the minstrel by the neck hem of his tunic before he could attempt to rush to his wife's side and make the situation even worse.

Robin had long wondered what sort of man would pay for his daughter to have a life of misery with the Sheriff of Nottingham. Now, taking a long hard look at the Baron de Bracy for the first time, he saw a hard-eyed, cold man staring towards the trees. He seemed tense, his walking steps short and stiff— as though he was consumed with anger—and he suffered from a pronounced limp. The Baron's dark beard was speckled with glinting grey that betrayed his advancing years, and every line on his face was positioned sloping downwards; his whole being seemed caught in what appeared to be a permanent frown.

Robin put a gentle restraining arm out to Alan, who had moved forward after wrenching himself free from Nasir's tunic-scrunching grip. 'If you rush out there now, Alan, you could easily get Mildred killed. Look closely, there is a knife held at her throat.'

Alan gasped, his eyes brimming with tears.

'It is too dangerous,' Nasir concurred, his eyes set firmly on the scene as the party of soldiers and their hostages came to a stuttering standstill. 'Look. They wait halfway between the forest and the abbey.'

'The Abbot was hiding something from you after all, Tuck.'

'So it would seem, Robin,' Tuck sighed, clearly disappointed at the Abbot's allegiance to Mildred's wicked parent, 'so it would seem.'

As they watched, they saw that the guard holding the Baron's daughter was keeping close to de Bracy's left side. Meanwhile, behind them, the soldier who had charge of Marion was taking no chances, for he held her arms firmly crossed behind her back.

There was no time for any of them to comment on the situation further, for a barking shout came across the dusky clearing, 'Show yourself, outlaw!

And bring that unholy friar and useless minstrel with you.'

Robin whirled around to Alan with an angry hiss. 'How does the Baron know you are here? Quickly, man—the truth!'

Alarmed by the outlaw's gritty tone, Alan blustered, 'He gave me no choice! I'm sorry! He said he would kill Mildred if I didn't bring you here, Robin. He *forced* me to fetch you. That's why I went to Sherwood. I didn't know you were already here. How was I to know that? Please, Robin! I *had* to save her. I thought you'd be fine. You're all so brave; you *always* win the day.'

Alan's spluttering confession was cut off by a roar of impatience from the Baron.

'I *command* you to come here, Hood!'

With no time to make plans, Robin mouthed an urgent order in hushed tones, 'Nasir, Much, keep watch. I don't think they know you're here too. Tuck, Alan, come with me… Let's go.'

They began walking at an even pace, neither rushing nor dawdling so they had time to take in the scene that greeted them. But Robin groaned aloud as Alan suddenly darted forwards. Breaking into a run, his act of bravado achieved nothing more than causing the Baron to burst into a mocking laughter.

'Can't wait to reach your wife, minstrel? Guards! Grab them all!'

Obeying instantly, the guards surrounded Robin, Alan, Marion, Mildred, the Abbot and Tuck— enclosing them at the heart of a well-defended circle.

From the safety of the trees, Much muttered a sudden and worrying thought, 'Nasir, do you think Alan will tell de Bracy that we're here too?'

'If he does,' Nasir grimaced, in reply, 'he will never sing another song. I will see to that. Come.'

Nasir drew his bow and crept forward, edging around the tress to get as near as possible to the others. Much followed close behind him, slingshot already in his hand. As they listened, they could hear Alan's soft, sing-song voice pleading with the Baron.

'Please, my Lord. You have Robin Hood now, a far greater prize than the two of us. Please let your daughter go. Nobody could love her like I do.'

'Quiet, minstrel!' barked the Baron, his lip curled in disgust at the balladeer. His nostrils flared as if even just the scent of the simpering minstrel turned his stomach, and he added, 'the Abbot and I have business to discuss.'

Spinning around to face the crumbled cleric, the Baron snapped, 'It's time we moved into the church. My daughter's future husband will be here soon; I assume you have no objection to performing the ceremony?'

Shocked, the Abbot stuttered, 'But, my Lord, your daughter is *already* married. She has a husband.'

'*Falsely* married,' the Baron replied, matter-of-factly. 'But the presence of her fake husband is a situation with which can deal swiftly, and I assume there will be no objections to marrying off a very recent widow.' De Bracy raised his arm towards his soldiers, 'Men, shoot the minstrel!'

'*No*, Father! You can't. I love him!' Mildred's cry of dismay rang out as a pair of guards stepped forward from the circle, each with a loaded crossbow, which they aimed at Alan. Mildred let out a piercing scream that resounded through the clearing like a knife cutting through flesh, as more soldiers seized hold of Alan's shoulders, forcing him to stay still.

The minstrel mumbled in bewilderment, his eyes wide with terror and shocked confusion, 'But, my Lord, you promised me…'

For a split second, de Bracy ignored Alan and

simply glared at his daughter, observing—with unconcealed disgust—the tears that slid down her ghost-white face.

The Baron's moment of hesitation was all Robin needed. 'Now!'

Seizing his chance, Herne's son kicked out at his guard, while Marion, Tuck and Mildred grappled against their captors as well.

'I must protest!' The Abbot, dismayed at being caught in the middle of such a battle, sent up the briefest silent prayer, before adopting his best sermonising tone, shouting, 'This is holy ground. How dare you—'

The cleric's pleas evaporated into the chaos that surrounded him as, from the trees, Nasir tried to aim his bow. But there was no way he could shoot the Baron—or any of the soldiers—without risking an innocent life.

Instead, using the outcry as cover, Nasir and Much moved fast to get closer and in position for a better aim. They were almost within safe shooting range of the Baron when a bellow from Friar Tuck caused them to falter to a halt and wait to see what would happen next.

'SILENCE!' Tuck threw his full weight behind his words, causing the guards to pause mid-strike.

It was said with such force and command that the soldiers froze, holding their weapons uneasily, as one the soldier's eyes darted to their master for further orders.

Taking advantage of their hesitation, the friar grabbed his chance. 'There is no need for violence to begin a new wedding, is there? Though I originally carried out the ceremony, I regret to have since discovered that I had been excommunicated by way of my outlawry.'

'I *knew* it!' the Baron snarled.

'There is, thus, no need to kill a husband who isn't a husband,' Tuck explained.

A fragile hush hung in the air as Mildred and Alan swapped horrified and terrified glances.

The Baron de Bracy took a second to process this merciful suggestion, before he waved a hand at his men for them to lower their weapons, 'Keep the prisoners enclosed.' Then, regarding Alan as if he was something unpleasant on the bottom of his boot— and clearly disappointed that he hadn't already seen his would-be son-in-law dispatched to Hell—the Baron snorted, 'Death is obviously too good for you, minstrel. I am sure you will enjoy being the first to wish Mildred well as she commences married life. Come, let us prepare for the wedding.'

Nasir and Much watched silently as all but four of the guards withdrew into the gatehouse. As soon as the abbey's doors banged shut, and the main party was out of sight, Nasir raised his bow.

'I will take the two men on the right. You shoot the two on the left.'

'*Which* left, Nasir? *Our* left or *theirs?*'

Smiling as Much waved his right hand, Nasir muttered, '*Ours*. Now, on my mark: one, two—'

The Saracen's countdown died on his lips, and he quickly tapped Much's bow so it pointed downwards.

'Wait. Horses.'

Much gasped in surprise as another familiar figure rode into view.

CHAPTER SEVEN

The Sheriff of Nottingham, his horse surrounded by the Baron's armed guards, dismounted. He felt his jellied legs almost giving way as he stood on the soft grass. They had ridden directly from Nottingham with only one brief stop to rest the horses, and he was his usual mix of scathing moans and venomous self-pity.

'In the name of Beelzebub, my head hurts! And I swear my body has moulded to the shape of this horse.'

Having vowed never to drink cheap claret again on at least four separate occasions during the ride north, Robert de Rainault did so for a fifth time as the Baron de Bracy's captain grunted a reply. He'd had enough of the Sheriff by the third moan. 'It's a good job we've arrived then, isn't?' he muttered. 'For us. *And* for you.'

Looking around, taking in the old stone structure, the Sheriff spluttered, '*Finally!*' before adding, 'Well, where *are* we, then? To what hideous hideaway have you dragged me against my will?'

'Welbeck Abbey,' replied the Captain, 'I will fetch the Baron.' Dismounting, the Captain passed the reins of his horse to the nearest soldier.

Openly amazed that a man like the Baron would want to spend any time at all in a religious building, the Sheriff studied the abbey's impressive exterior. 'He's *here?* Why?'

The Captain smirked as the door to the abbey was thrown open, and the Baron de Bracy himself— flanked by two armed guards—came out to greet them.

'Ah! The bridegroom has arrived. Well done, Captain.'

'My Lord,' the Captain bowed as de Bracy limped towards them, his stick thumping on the ground.

A flutter of alarm stirred in the Sheriff's stomach as he mumbled to himself, '*Bridegroom?*'

As the Baron approached closer, De Rainault managed to contort an impression of pleasure onto his face. 'My Lord de Bracy, this is a nice surprise.'

'*Is* it De Rainault? Are you *sure?*'

'Of course, it's always a pleasure to—'

Cutting across him, the Baron spoke with a firm satisfaction that filled the Sheriff with a sense of dread. 'Now everyone who attempted to humiliate the proud name of de Bracy is here! You are just in time for your wedding, Sheriff. After all, you've already had the dowry… and spent it on wine and jewels, if I know you.'

De Rainault's eyes darted about in panic. On the journey he had cooked up—and dismissed—dozens of explanations as to what *might* have happened to the dowry. But now, face-to-face with William de Bracy, and surrounded by men brandishing swords and crossbows, the Sheriff could only bluster, 'My Lord, there has been a terrible misunderstanding! Robin Hood must have tricked you into thinking that I—'

'Silence! You are to marry my daughter.'

As two guards stepped up to station themselves either side of him, the Sheriff of Nottingham resigned himself to his fate as a thought crossed his mind. *I suppose I could always send Mildred to live with Abbot Hugo. I would, at least, enjoy how much he'd hate that.*

Still watching from the shelter of the trees, Nasir narrowed his eyes as the Sheriff and the Baron reached the threshold of the gatehouse. 'Ready with your bow, Much?'

'Ready.'

'Good.' Nasir drew his bow back. 'After me.'

'More outlaws!' came the cry, as an arrow buried itself deeply into the door of the gatehouse. The Baron yelled out in terror, 'Men!'

There was no time for his soldiers to respond, however, for Much's arrow had struck its target perfectly; it sat squarely in the Baron's leg—the same leg that had been wounded prior to Mildred's sham marriage and which had never properly healed.

Screaming in shock and pain, de Bracy almost fainted as he fell to the ground. More arrows flew over him, whistling across the clearing.

As one of the men-at-arms crumpled to the ground with a sickening thud and an arrow in his back, more soldiers ran from the abbey, holding their prisoners before as human shields. Amid the chaos, the Captain yelled, 'The Baron's been shot! Men! Forward!'

More arrows flew, and a second soldier thudded onto the grass as the Sheriff scrambled to get away, forgetting all his qualms about going inside the abbey to become a married man. 'Out of my way, out of my way! *Sanctuary!*'

The Captain, however, had other ideas. 'Where do you think you're going, Sheriff?'

De Rainault stuttered in surprise when, finally looking up at the melee, he saw a familiar man being thrust out of the doorway, and straight into his path. 'Wait… that's… Robin Hood? What the devil is going on?'

The Sheriff's sickly pallor paled further as he saw Much and Nasir running across the clearing.

Within seconds, the Sheriff witnessed Herne's son break free from his captors and, without hesitation, throw a heavy punch that sent one of the guards flailing to the ground.

'Much! Get to the Baron. Hold him down.'

Obeying Robin instantly, Much—pulling out his dagger whilst he ran—launched himself heavily onto the Baron's chest. The wounded nobleman cried out in pain as he was pinned to the floor, a blade at his throat.

Meanwhile, as her friends fought around her, Marion managed to wrestle herself free. With a sharp kick at the nearest soldier's knee, she ran towards Tuck, who was battling hard to escape the grip of the guard who still held his wrists behind his back. Elbowing the soldier squarely in the face, Marion toppled him backwards, leaving him sprawled across the floor.

'Thank you, Little Flower—' Tuck broke off, 'Robin! Duck, there's—'

There was another thud as Robin ducked, then swung upwards, connecting his fist with another solider, who he toppled off his feet.

'Thanks, Tuck!' Robin shouted, as he turned in time to see Nasir running in their direction.

Throwing two knives as he moved, the Saracen's weapons each met their target —one soldier per blade—with a sickeningly quiet hum. He only stopped on reaching De Rainault, where he drew his twin swords.

'Hello, Sheriff. Fancy a haircut?'

The Sheriff gulped, 'Nasir.'

Before De Rainault received an unwanted trim, Robin yelled, 'ENOUGH!'

Instantly, the guards' weapons were thrown to the ground; they knew when they were beaten, especially with their employer pinned to the ground and a knife at his throat.

Marion, Tuck, Nasir and Much watched each figure carefully as they closed in around them. The tide had turned; captors had become prisoners.

An uneasy hush fell across the clearing as Mildred ran to her father's side. 'How could you *do* this?' she cried.

His face etched with pain, the Baron still managed to snarl at his only child, 'And how could *you* disgrace me so?'

Much shuffled off the Baron's chest as Mildred used the hem of her gown to stem the trickle of blood which leaked from his wound. She was suddenly quite calm, as she took in the situation. 'That arrow needs to come out, Father. It will hurt, and the wound will take a long time to heal. Longer perhaps than the one from which you already suffer.'

The Baron winced at the thought of the arrow being removed from his leg—and at the thought of such a long recovery. Mildred saw the worry flit across his features.

'If you accept Alan as my husband,' she said, 'then I will come and care for you until you are well.'

The Baron coughed, speaking slowly as a new wave of pain flowed through him, 'And what if I refuse to let a daughter who abandoned her family and her duty—for something as pointless as love nonetheless—tend to my wounds?'

'Then, this is where I accept that you'd rather see me unhappy than have your pride hurt. And this will become the moment when I say goodbye for good. You can go back to your castle, father. Alone. Alone and with no one to care for you but your steward, your falcons and your hounds. Or...'

Through clenched teeth, de Bracy muttered, 'You are no daughter of mine.'

Standing back up, staring down at her father's broken body and gaining a new steely resolve, Mildred pointed an accusing finger at Robert De Rainault. 'Then, Father, it won't matter to you that I am never ever going to marry *that* sorry excuse for a man.'

The Sheriff, unsure if he was more terrified at viewing the world from the sharp end of Nasir's blades or relieved that—thanks to the outlaws—he'd been spared marriage to the girl for a second time, gaped open-mouthed, unable to believe it all.

Meanwhile, Robin found that he was only just resisting the urge to kick some sense into the man lying on the ground. 'You're a proud and foolish man, Baron! You don't deserve such a kind-hearted child. Most would have left you to rot without so much as a backward glance, let alone an offer of help.'

Another moan of pain shot from the fallen man's lips. He closed his eyes, turning his face from both his daughter and the outlaw who had thwarted his plans for him to marry her off.

'I'm tempted to leave that arrow in your leg, but as I have no wish for an arrow of ours to kill anyone if I can prevent it, then I'm going to pull it out.' Robin shook his head. 'Tuck, Much, hold the Baron's shoulders.'

Grasping hold of the shaft of the arrow sticking out of the nobleman's leg, Robin waited as Nasir added his weight to hold down the Baron's healthy leg. Then, with a shout of, 'NOW!' Robin yanked the missile free with one smooth tug.

The Baron's initial sickening scream soon turned into raggedly heavy, agonised panting. Eventually, as Tuck wiped the dots of perspiration from his patient's brow, the Baron spoke, biting off every begrudging word. 'I will allow her to keep her minstrel… but *only* if the Sheriff repays the dowry.' he almost cried out again, in agony, but swallowed it and—through gritted teeth—barked, 'In God's name… someone get me a strong drink!'

Robert de Rainault bustled to the Baron's side, showcasing his usual flip-flopping personality, which ranged from sarcastic sneering—when he had the upper hand—to contrite hand-wringing when he didn't. 'Of course, of course,' he simpered, 'it was all just a misunderstanding anyway, and—'

Darting forward, Robin grabbed the Sheriff of Nottingham's arm, squeezing it hard, an unyielding expression on his face. '—and *you*, Sheriff, will find that money *without* taking a single penny from the people. I will be watching you… *very* carefully indeed.'

CHAPTER EIGHT

'What's that noise?' asked Will Scarlet, nudging Little John in the ribs. 'Horses?'

Little John silently rotated on the spot. He nodded as the faint sound of a hooves was carried on the wind towards them. 'Nasir would be able to tell us how many there are.'

'He ain't 'ere, so I'm guessing *for* him—and I guess three. You?'

'Sounds about right.'

'You've got to guess an exact amount. It's a wager.'

'A wager? What's the prize?'

'Whoever guesses right gets to try and shave Nasir's moustache off when he's asleep.'

'Not for me, lad. He'd slit your throat the moment you touched his skin!'

'Nah, I reckon I could, John.'

'He's a light sleeper.'

'Oh, did I say "asleep"? I meant after accidentally knocking him out cold when he wasn't looking.'

Little John chuckled. 'Come on, then. Let's get under cover and see.'

As the two outlaws moved into the cover of a nearby cluster of young ash trees where their trap was baited, Will notched an arrow onto his bow. 'You ready for this, John?'

'I'm ready. I just hope that rope holds and this plan of yours works.'

'Well, if it don't, we'll not stay alive long enough to find out.'

'It might *not* be Gisburne, of course,' John whispered.

'And if it ain't, we won't use the rope! Plus, we've got that wager. I still say three horses.'

John was about to reply, when Sir Guy and three men-at-arms rode into view. 'I'd say four horses!' he quickly whispered, grinning.

'No deal!' hissed back Scarlet, 'You saw them!'

Moving in single file, they were heading to the village via the widest trackway, just as Will had said they would. A trackway that—for a few metres in one particular section—became very narrow indeed.

'Hard, fast and final, right? Then we get outta 'ere,' Scarlet muttered, as he aimed an arrow at the last rider in the row.

'Yes, hard and fast—but not final, Will. We can't *kill* Gisburne.'

'We bloody well should'

'We don't need the Sheriff immediately after us for his death, certainly not whilst we're on our own here. No doubt *his Lordship* will have been told about Meg and Wickham too, and that would be his way in to get his revenge on us, for killing Gisburne, I would expect.'

'And Robin would kill us anyway for not letting *him* dispatch Gisburne,' Scarlet added. He could just imagine the look on Robin's face if they told him they'd taken out the Sheriff's deputy. 'Just hard and fast, then—this time. I hope you tied that rope tight enough.'

'I did my best, Will. Now shut yer yapping, they're getting closer.' Raising his knife to where he'd attached one end of the straining rope to the nearest pliant tree trunk, hoping that they'd created enough tension in it for their plan to work, Little John waited for Will Scarlet to let loose his arrow.

'Hold it... not until they're at the narrowest point of the path. Almost... One, two, three... *Now!*'

Scarlet's arrow hit its mark, as the soldier behind Gisburne fell to the ground with a strangled cry, and Sir Guy's yell of, 'Outlaws!' resounded across Sherwood.

John sawed through the rope with his knife, working fast, sweat dotting his forehead as they saw Gisburne and his surviving men come to a standstill.

Will shot again, and the first soldier in the row joined his colleague on the forest floor.

'Hood! Show yourself!' Unable to turn around—wedged as he and his guard were in the confined space, trapped further by the bodies of a fallen soldier before and behind them—and with their horses stamping and whinnying, Gisburne, stood tall in his stirrups, craning to see into the trees. 'I said, show yourselves, outlaw scum!'

John's knife, still sawing furiously back and forth in his large palm, was almost through the last few frays of rope. 'Any... second... Get ready, Will... Now!'

As the blade severed the tightly tied rope, Will Scarlet and Little John ducked to the ground just in time as it sprang free, lashing forwards like a whip, its free end whizzing over their heads.

Little John winced as the rope made a whip-crack sound when it collided with the two hapless horsemen, sending Gisburne and his surviving soldier flying. Their screams as they were catapulted into the air were accompanied by the panic of the four horses which reared and scattered, making their way into the forest as fast as they could.

Wasting no time, the two outlaws broke cover and dashed to the fallen men. Both were out cold.

'Thank goodness for that!' Scarlet wiped a hand over his forehead. 'Now, let's get them trussed up, then at least we know they won't be able to cause any trouble until we get back.'

'And I can stop worrying about Meg for a while.'

Will rolled his eyes. 'Chance would be a fine thing, John; chance would be a fine thing!'

Resting against the abbey's solid stone wall, the outlaws watched as the Sheriff of Nottingham leapt onto his horse, with an emphasis on speed rather than dignity. He urged his mount into a gallop and left without a backward glance.

The remainder of the men-at-arms took no notice of the fleeing nobleman as they placed their fallen comrades into the back of a cart, whilst two monks from the abbey leant a hand to lay the injured baron carefully onto a litter. As soon as de Bracy was as comfortable as his leg and wounded pride would allow, the depleted party rode away—the earlier atmosphere of gloom and fear departing with them.

Once the convoy had completely disappeared from view, the Abbot of Welbeck, his expression sombre with regret, approached Tuck. 'Thank the Lord they've gone. I owe you a sincere apology.'

The friar pulled his cloak around his shoulders. 'No, you owe Mildred and Alan an apology. You owe the rest of us an explanation.'

Diving his cold hands deep into his habit, the Abbot grimaced. 'I am ashamed to say, I do. The Baron learnt that I had given the king's taxes to the poor. He threatened to report me to the Crown. If I didn't do as he said, I'd have lost my position here. Can you imagine with whom King John might have replaced me?'

Tuck placed a comforting hand on the older man's shoulder. 'Yes, I can. A man bent more to the King's own way of thinking, I suspect.'

'Exactly. I was afraid of what would happen to my people. I'm sorry.'

'No need for an apology. Your explanation is a

sound one,' Robin came forward, understanding the Abbot's predicament.

The Abbot looked longingly towards the safety—and the peace and quiet—afforded by his abbey. 'Perhaps we should go inside and consider this young couple's situation in case the friar here was right?'

Tuck wiped a trickle of sweat from his tonsure, 'In case I was right? Right about what?'

'I don't know personally if you *have* been excommunicated, Friar. And neither do *you*. Isn't it better that these young people are married twice— to make sure they are truly wed—than not at all? It's the least I can do to make amends for what the Baron initially persuaded me to do. Come on, let's all go inside.'

Their assembled boots and sandals clattered across the stone as they passed through the gatehouse and into the main body of the abbey. As they made their way across the hall towards the church, Robin paused. 'What's that?'

Following the outlaw's line of sight, the Abbot

said, 'The Baron threw our shield to the ground in a fit of anger.'

'Not the shield, the little thing next to it.' Bending down, he picked up a small band of gold that had been lying on the stone floor next to the fallen shield.

Marion beamed. 'It's their betrothal ring!'

Robin placed the small circle of gold in the palm of his hand and lifted it up in the candlelight. 'Alan, Mildred; you're going to need this.'

As the bell to evening prayers sounded, the outlaws gathered outside the abbey and said their goodbyes.

'Are you sure you won't stay until morning? It isn't always safe to travel at night in the forest.'

'I suspect we'll be alright, Father,' Robin smiled.

The Abbot blushed as he saw the knowing expressions on the outlaw's face and realised the faux pas he'd just made. 'Forgive me, Robin. Again. I forgot who I was I talking to.' He turned to Alan and Mildred, 'You two will stay tonight, perhaps?'

Alan bowed gracefully. 'Thank you, my Lord Abbot. We will.'

Mildred, ring shining anew on her finger, agreed, 'A night's rest before we begin the long ride back to Scotland would be most welcome.'

Robin hooked his bow over his shoulder. 'Still believe love conquerors all then, Alan?'

'I *know* it does, Robin. After all,' he pulled his wife to his side, embracing her as he did so, 'I've got Mildred back, which proves it.'

Robin only just resisted the urge to shake his head. Alan a Dale was a dreamer, he'd never understand the battles they faced everyday just to stay alive, but perhaps ignorance was bliss, in his case at least.

Blushing like the new bride she was, again, Mildred hugged Marion before addressing the outlaws, 'Thank you. All of you.'

'You are welcome; but it's time for us to say goodbye.' Robin suddenly felt impatient to return to the heart of Sherwood. 'We need to get back to Little John and Will.'

As the outlaws faced the forest, looking forward to being reunited with their friends, Marion gave the happy couple one last hug. 'You play the lute as well as sing, don't you, Alan?'

'Yes, why?'

'Maybe, in the future, you might play the music and let your wife do the singing?'

EPILOGUE

'There you are!' John beamed, as he saw his fellow outlaws appear through the trees only two hours after he and Will Scarlet had left Wickham.

'Yeah,' Scarlet gave Much a playful poke in the ribs, 'you've been gone so long, we were on our way to rescue you.'

'Oh yeah,' Robin chuckled as their friends fell into step with them, 'and there I was wondering if we'd arrive back to find you two needing rescuing from Gisburne.'

'No chance of that,' Will winked, 'he won't be causing any trouble tonight.'

'Why so sure, Will?' Marion grinned as she gave him a suspicious look.

'Let's just say, he's a bit tied up at the moment.'

As night drew in, the outlaws lapsed into a companionable silence. A cloudy grey mist had taken a firm hold on the forest as they wandered deeper into the comforting dark shadows that blanketed their home.

They were almost back at their camp when Much increased his pace so he could walk at Robin's side.

'Robin, Nasir heard Alan singing about *us*.'

'Really?'

'Yes, he was singing songs about us fighting for the poor. Should he be doing that?'

'I wouldn't worry, Much.' Robin slapped him on the back. 'Alan's a kind-hearted man, but not a very good minstrel. Most of his audience will have their ears covered.'

Much grinned, 'And we'll be safe from him informing too many people about what we do and where we hide out!' he added, relieved.

'We will, Much. And, anyway, I can't imagine ballads about *us* ever being too popular—can you?'

Also from Chinbeard and Oak Tree Books

www.ingramcontent.com/pod-product-compliance
Lightning Source LLC
Chambersburg PA
CBHW011438170626
46808CB00009B/3104